FI

HOW THE ANIMALS GOT THEIR COLORS

Animal Myths from around the World

MICHAEL ROSEN

illustrated by
John Clementson

HARCOURT BRACE JOVANOVICH, PUBLISHERS
SAN DIEGO   NEW YORK   LONDON

STORYTELLER'S NOTE

From the beginning of recorded time, people have been telling each other stories. Thousands of tales have been told and retold around the world to answer a multitude of questions: Why does the sun rise each day? Why are there rainbows? How did animals get their colors?

Many of these stories take place long, long ago in a time before humans were born when gods ruled the earth and had the power to change and create animals. People told these stories to their children, who told them to their children, and so they were passed on to us. The people believed these tales and lived by their truths and teachings. They used them as explanation and celebration of the natural world, and often dances and ceremonies grew around the tales and their telling.

Today we may call these stories myths, but they were vital to earlier people and taught respect and admiration for the powers of animals and nature. These tales have survived changing times and cultures, and they have much to reveal about life, humor, and the roles all creatures play in the balance of the world.

CONTENTS

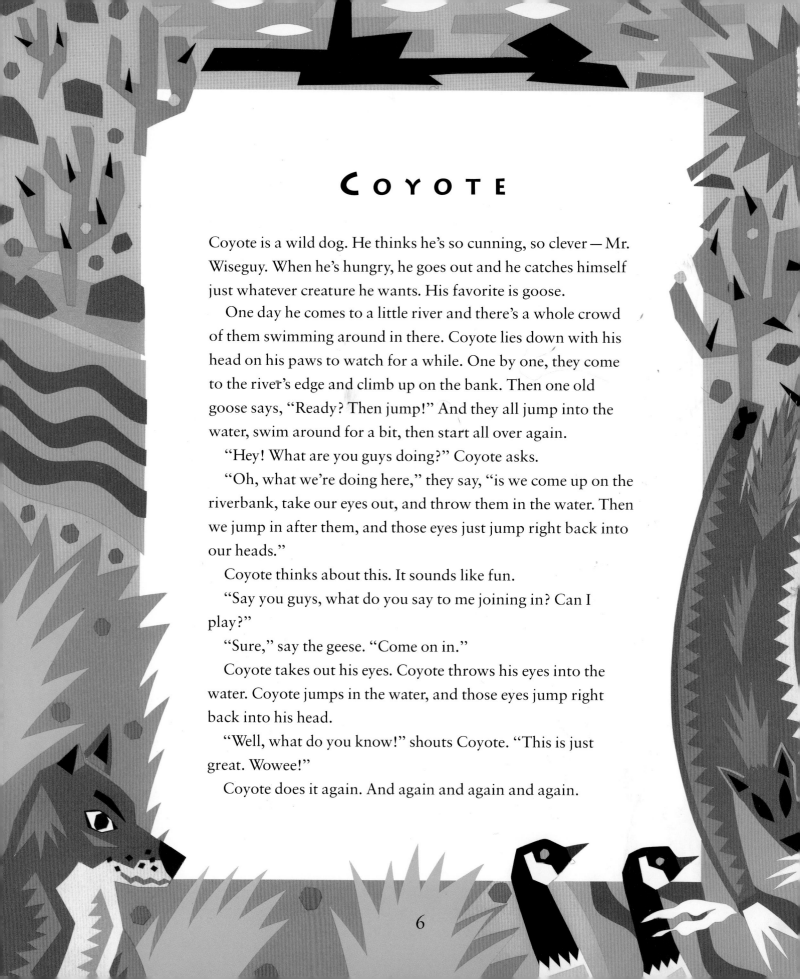

COYOTE

Coyote is a wild dog. He thinks he's so cunning, so clever — Mr. Wiseguy. When he's hungry, he goes out and he catches himself just whatever creature he wants. His favorite is goose.

One day he comes to a little river and there's a whole crowd of them swimming around in there. Coyote lies down with his head on his paws to watch for a while. One by one, they come to the river's edge and climb up on the bank. Then one old goose says, "Ready? Then jump!" And they all jump into the water, swim around for a bit, then start all over again.

"Hey! What are you guys doing?" Coyote asks.

"Oh, what we're doing here," they say, "is we come up on the riverbank, take our eyes out, and throw them in the water. Then we jump in after them, and those eyes just jump right back into our heads."

Coyote thinks about this. It sounds like fun.

"Say you guys, what do you say to me joining in? Can I play?"

"Sure," say the geese. "Come on in."

Coyote takes out his eyes. Coyote throws his eyes into the water. Coyote jumps in the water, and those eyes jump right back into his head.

"Well, what do you know!" shouts Coyote. "This is just great. Wowee!"

Coyote does it again. And again and again and again.

6

Women went out and found them, fished for them. In the people's gardens, weeds grew and smothered the roots and berries the people used to eat.

But the women fished on and on. From the sound of the first bird of morning until the sun set in the sea, they fished for flying fish.

The old man saw that soon there would be no fish left. He went among the fish saying, "Go, go and live far out at sea, and we will seek you out only when the time is right."

But the flying fish stayed, sinking deeper into the mud to keep from the women's sight.

So the old man took up pieces of broken coral and hurled them at the flying fish, "Go now if you want to live. Go now, so we may always have flying fish to hunt."

When the pieces of broken coral hit the flying fish, they took off and fled from the old man, taking themselves far out to sea.

Look now at the flying fish, and you will see pink marks on their heads made by the coral the old man threw when he first sent them far out to sea.

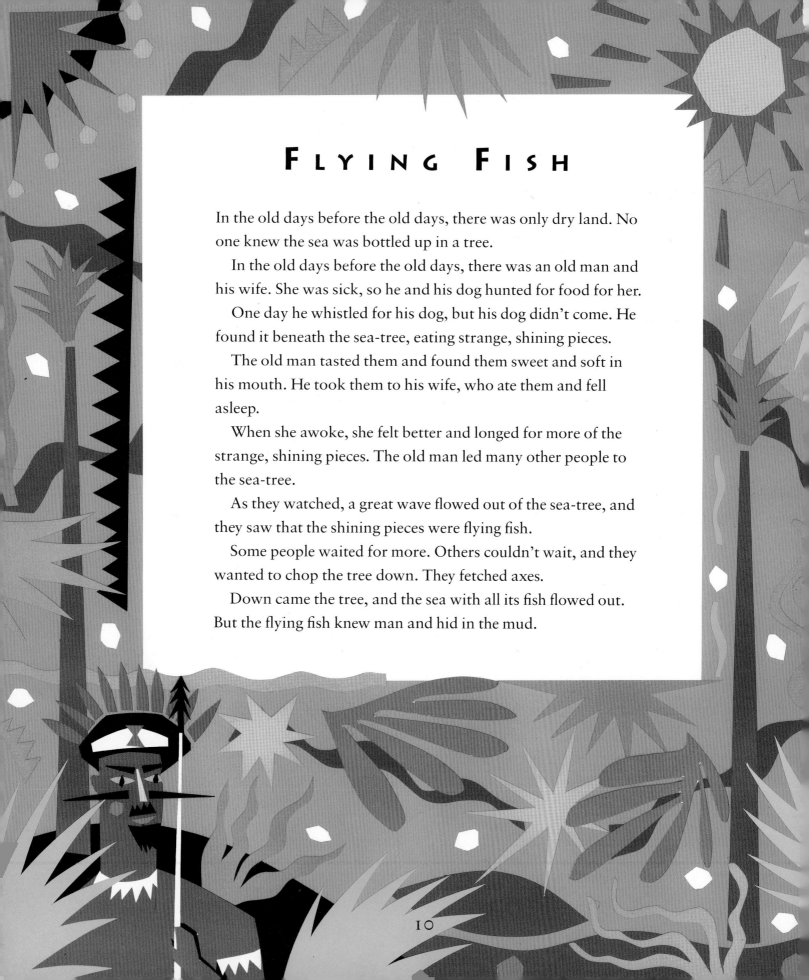

FLYING FISH

In the old days before the old days, there was only dry land. No one knew the sea was bottled up in a tree.

In the old days before the old days, there was an old man and his wife. She was sick, so he and his dog hunted for food for her.

One day he whistled for his dog, but his dog didn't come. He found it beneath the sea-tree, eating strange, shining pieces.

The old man tasted them and found them sweet and soft in his mouth. He took them to his wife, who ate them and fell asleep.

When she awoke, she felt better and longed for more of the strange, shining pieces. The old man led many other people to the sea-tree.

As they watched, a great wave flowed out of the sea-tree, and they saw that the shining pieces were flying fish.

Some people waited for more. Others couldn't wait, and they wanted to chop the tree down. They fetched axes.

Down came the tree, and the sea with all its fish flowed out. But the flying fish knew man and hid in the mud.

"Wowee! This is just about the best bit of fun I've had in years," he says.

But the geese start getting tired of him. There's no need to get quite so excited about it, they think. All we're doing is taking our eyes out, throwing them in the river, and jumping in after them. No big deal.

"Hey, what do you say to this?" says one goose, real quiet to his friend. "When Coyote throws his eyes in, we get in there and steal them."

"Nice," says his friend. "I like it."

Coyote throws in his eyes. "Wowee! There they go again," he shouts.

And just as quick as you like, the geese whip those eyes out of the water, and they're off, away.

Coyote jumps in. No eyes. His eyes aren't there. They don't jump back into his head.

"Aieee, geese! You've tricked me. You don't want me to see, right? I get it. Steal his eyes and old Coyote won't know where he is, right? Well, listen here, geese. I'm coming after you, and I'm going to eat you up, from top to toe. Every little feather on your heads."

"Come get us then, Coyote. Come get us," shout the geese.

Up jumps Coyote. He's out of the river, and he's running down the riverbank after them. But the river turns, and next

thing he's back in the river. He can't see a thing.

"I'll catch them," says Coyote. He reaches down and finds a couple of pebbles. He puts them in his eyeholes.

"I can see you now," he shouts. "At least, I will in just a moment," he mutters to himself as he fiddles with the pebbles, trying to make them work like eyes. But nothing. They don't work, and they drop out. On he runs. Round and round. Seeing nothing, finding nothing, until he bumps right into a cactus.

"Aieee," shouts Coyote. "Cactus! Ah . . . cactus. I know cactus with the big yellow berries. Find one, Coyote, find one."

So Coyote feels over the cactus with his paw. The prickles hurt.

"Aieee, it must be here, there must be one." And sure enough, Coyote finds a big yellow cactus berry. He puts it in his eyehole.

"Hey, I can see. Coyote, that was smart. Now just find another one to match."

Off goes Coyote again, the one cactus-berry eye in his head, looking for more cactus berries. And he finds one. Puts it in. Two yellow eyes.

"Now for the geese," he says.

But the geese are gone. Not one in sight. And off goes Coyote, hunting those geese. And he's still out there hunting them today. Now you know why. And something else: Now you know how he got those angry yellow eyes.

HOW THE ANIMALS
GOT THEIR COLORS

To Geraldine, Joe, Naomi, Eddie, Laura, and Isaac
— M. R.

To my family, with special thanks to Miriam
— J. C.

Text copyright © 1992, 1991 by Michael Rosen
Illustrations copyright © 1992, 1991 by John Clementson

First published 1991 by Studio Editions Limited
First U.S. edition 1992

Requests for permission to make copies of any
part of the work should be mailed to:
Permissions Department,
Harcourt Brace Jovanovich, Publishers, 8th Floor,
Orlando, Florida 32887.

Library of Congress Cataloging-in-Publication Data
Rosen, Michael, 1946–
How the animals got their colors: animal myths
from around the world/by Michael Rosen:
illustrated by John Clementson — 1st ed.
p.   cm.
Originally published: London, England:
Studio Editions, 1991.
Summary: A collection of tales from around the
world explaining how various animals got their colors.
ISBN 0-15-236783-7
1. Tales [1. Folklore.   2. Animals—Folklore.]
I. Clementson, John, ill.   II. Title.
PZ8.1.R6837Ho   1992
398.2—dc20   91-30113   [E]
Printed in Hong Kong
A B C D E

Sources

Leopard: *Folk Tales From Liberia*. Richard Bundy, U.S. Legation to
Liberia. Reproduced by permission of the American Folklore Society
from the *Journal of American Folklore* 31:121, 1918. Not for sale or
further reproduction.
Brolga: Adapted from *The Dawn of Time — Australian Aboriginal
Myths*. Ainslie Roberts and Charles P. Mountford (Art Australia, Aus-
tralia, 1989).
Coyote: *Zuni Tales*. Edward Handy. Reproduced by permission of the
American Folklore Society from the *Journal of American Folklore*
32:125, 1919. Not for sale or further reproduction.
Frog: *The Golden Age of Myth and Fable*. Thomas Bulfinch (Bracken
Books, London, 1985).
Crane: *The King of the Snakes*. Rosetta Baskerville (Sheldon Press,
Uganda, 1922).
Peacock: *Folk Tales of the Khasis*. Mrs. Rafy (Macmillan, London,
1920).
Flying Fish: *Papuan Fairy Tales*. Annie Kerr (Macmillan, London,
1910).
Tiger: *Songs and Stories of the Chu'an Miao*. David Crockett Graham
(Smithsonian Institution, Washington DC, 1954).
How the Animals Got Their Colors: *Folk Literature of the Ayoreo
Indians*. ed. Johannes Wilbert and Karin Simoneau (*UCLA Latin
American Studies,* Vol. 70, 1989).

10/92

FROG

Back in the days when people knew gods and goddesses could come down to earth and their children walked among us, Latona, a daughter of the gods, was hurrying through some woods, carrying her two babies. She was looking for somewhere to rest; somewhere she could find fresh water to drink, for she and her children had mouths as dry as dust. Her eyes fell on some country people hard at work, gathering reeds to make baskets. Close by them was a pool of lovely clear water.

Latona ran to the waterside, knelt down, and just as she was about to feel the cool, wet taste on her tongue, the country people stopped her.

"No! Drinking from this water is not allowed," the country people said.

Latona was furious. "Not allowed? Water is like the air and sunshine — it is free for all to use, and I have come to take my share. And listen, I won't wash in it, I won't bathe my tired legs in it, I won't stir up the mud. All I want is to quench my thirst. My mouth is so dry, I can hardly speak. One taste of this water would be heaven. Can't you see my little children stretching out their arms, begging for water?"

But the country people wouldn't move. "The water is not for you. If we let any old tramp come here and drink, there'd be none left for us. Now clear off!"

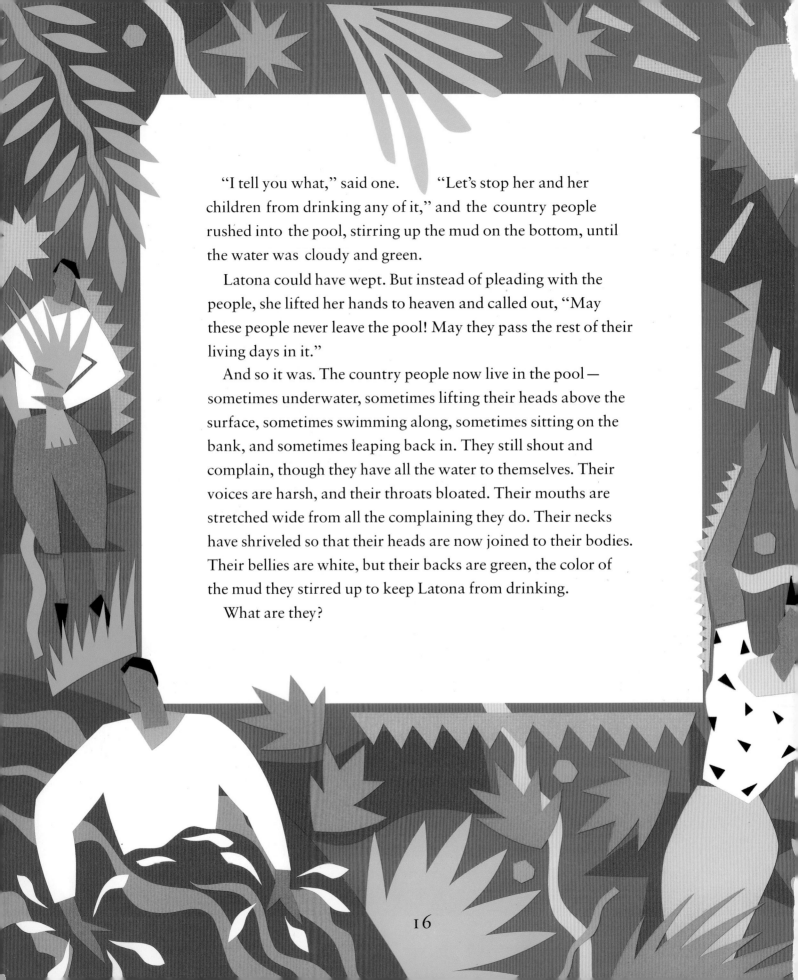

"I tell you what," said one. "Let's stop her and her children from drinking any of it," and the country people rushed into the pool, stirring up the mud on the bottom, until the water was cloudy and green.

Latona could have wept. But instead of pleading with the people, she lifted her hands to heaven and called out, "May these people never leave the pool! May they pass the rest of their living days in it."

And so it was. The country people now live in the pool — sometimes underwater, sometimes lifting their heads above the surface, sometimes swimming along, sometimes sitting on the bank, and sometimes leaping back in. They still shout and complain, though they have all the water to themselves. Their voices are harsh, and their throats bloated. Their mouths are stretched wide from all the complaining they do. Their necks have shriveled so that their heads are now joined to their bodies. Their bellies are white, but their backs are green, the color of the mud they stirred up to keep Latona from drinking.

What are they?

TIGER

A meeting is taking place on Great Mountain.

Tiger says Tiger's the best, the strongest, the fastest on earth. Thunder says Thunder's the best, the loudest, the fiercest on earth. Echo says Echo's the best, the toughest, the cleverest on earth. Dragon says Dragon's the best, the mightiest, the hottest on earth.

"Yes, yes, yes," says Tiger, "I know all about you. But the thing that makes me the best is I'm not afraid of anything."

Tiger, Thunder, Echo, and Dragon cannot decide who is the greatest.

"Let us have a contest," says Tiger. "In this contest we will see which of us is the most terrifying. Whoever can make the other three cry, 'Stop, no more!' is the winner."

They all agree, and Tiger laughs.

"Now I'll show them."

Tiger paws the ground, opens his jaws, shows every tooth in his head, and roars. Thunder vanishes into thin air and sits among the clouds. Echo rolls down Great Mountain, across Blue River, up Little Mountain and is gone. Dragon coils and twists her long body and tail and squirms her way up into the sky, out of reach of Tiger's claws.

No one cries, "Stop, no more!" Tiger is left pawing the ground and roaring to himself until no roar is left. Thunder, Echo, and Dragon come back.

"Tiger loses," they say.

"I know, I know, I know," says Tiger.

Now Thunder comes forward, looks around at the clouds, and flies off to the deepest, darkest one in sight. From that cloud comes the most horrendous drumming and deafening rolls.

Tiger can't bear it and shouts, "Stop, no more!"

But Echo listens to Thunder's rolls, waits for them at the top of Little Mountain, and rolls them back at Thunder. And Dragon just coils and twists her long body and tail and squirms her way up into the sky, up above Thunder's clouds where it is all quiet.

Thunder, Echo, and Dragon come back.

"Thunder loses," they say.

"I'm better than Tiger," says Thunder.

"I know, I know, I know," says Tiger.

Now Echo comes forward and waits.

"Well, aren't you going to start?" says Tiger.

"Going to start?" says Echo.

"Well, don't hang about," says Tiger.

"Don't hang about," says Echo.

"It's not me that's hanging about, you fool," says Tiger.

"You fool," says Echo.

"Who are you calling a fool?" asks Tiger angrily.

"Who are you calling a fool?" asks Echo angrily.

"You," says Tiger.

"You," says Echo.

"Just get on with it," roars Tiger.

"Get on with it," roars Echo.

"It's not my turn," says Tiger.

"It's not my turn," says Echo.

"It is," shouts Tiger.

"It is," shouts Echo.

"You're driving me mad," says Tiger.

"You're driving me mad," says Echo.

"Stop, stop, no more!" cries Tiger.

"Stop, stop, no more!" cries Echo.

"I agree," says Thunder.

"I agree," says Echo.

"Stop, no more!" says Thunder.

Echo looks around for Dragon, but Dragon has coiled and twisted up her long body and tail and squirmed away up into the sky, where not even an echo can reach. Sometime later, Dragon comes back.

"Echo loses," they say.

"Echo was better than Thunder," says Dragon.

"Better than Thunder," says Echo.

"That's true," says Thunder.

"Echo was better than Tiger," says Dragon.

"Better than Tiger," says Echo.

"I know, I know, I know," says Tiger.

Now it's Dragon's turn. Dragon coils and twists her long body and tail and pours fire out of her mouth. Thunder flees to a cloud, but Dragon follows and breathes fire on the cloud and dries it up until there is nowhere for Thunder to sit.

"Stop, no more!" shouts Thunder.

Dragon chases Echo down Great Mountain, across Blue River, and up Little Mountain until they meet going down the other side.

"Do you want to give up?" asks Dragon.

"Give up," says Echo.

"Stop, no more?" asks Dragon.

"Stop, no more," says Echo.

"And now for Tiger," says Dragon. But Tiger is hiding in the forest on the side of the Great Mountain. So Dragon coils and twists up her long body and tail and lets fly a huge jet of flame, setting that forest on fire. But Tiger is ready, and he runs from the fire that races through the trees. And Tiger could have escaped, but for the wind in the treetops that flies even faster. Just as Tiger is leaving the forest, the fire crackles overhead. Flaming branches of a tree fall on Tiger, just as he thinks he is free.

"Stop, no more!" shouts Tiger.

"I've won," says Dragon.

"That's true," say Thunder and Echo.

"Never mind that," says Tiger, "look at my coat, the branches have burned my fur."

"Yes," says Dragon. "You're all stripy."

"I know, I know, I know," says Tiger.

B R O L G A

No one could dance like Brolga.
No one could dance like Brolga.

Everyone came to see her dancing. The women beat the ground to the rhythm of her steps. The men danced along with her and, one by one, stepped forward hoping to marry her.

One was Nonega. He was evil. He could make magic. How he wanted to marry her! But the old men of the tribe said no. They didn't want Brolga to marry anyone so evil.

"If I can't have Brolga," said Nonega, "Then no one else will."

No one could dance like Brolga.
No one could dance like Brolga.

One day Brolga danced on her own out on the plain. But a whirlwind came rushing toward her, nearer and nearer, and in the middle of the whirlwind was Nonega. As it roared across the plain, it sucked up dry dust into itself. The air whirled faster and faster over Brolga's face until the whirlwind was upon her. It wrapped itself around her until she disappeared into the cloud of dust.

For a while the whirlwind twisted there, then it passed on. There was no sign of Brolga. But in her place stood a tall bird, as gray as the whirlwind's dust. It swayed and waved its wings just as Brolga had danced.

When the people saw the bird, they called out, "Brolga! Brolga!"

The bird seemed to hear them and danced and danced while the women beat the ground to the rhythm of its steps.

And a tall bird can still be seen out on the plains of Northern Australia, swaying and waving its wings, with feathers as gray as a whirlwind's dust.

No one could dance like Brolga.
No one could dance like Brolga.

LEOPARD

See Leopard. He can leap so quick he's out of sight before you've blinked. Watch him.

See Nyomo. His eyes are so good, he can stand at the bottom of a tree and see a fly on the topmost leaf. Watch him.

You've heard of Lion? Wait for him. He comes later.

One day Leopard says to Nyomo, "Let's go, you and me, and find wild honey."

They walk. Leopard's paws pad on the ground. *Foop, foop, foop.* Nyomo's feet glide beside Leopard. *Shoo, shoo, shoo.*

"Look there!" says Leopard. "A bees' nest. I am the first to see a nest full of honey!"

They look inside. "No honey," says Nyomo. "Walk on."

They walk. *Foop, foop, foop* go Leopard's paws. *Shoo, shoo, shoo* go Nyomo's feet.

"Look there!" says Nyomo. "A bees' nest. I am the first to see a nest full of honey!"

They look inside. "Honey!" says Nyomo. "Let's eat."

They eat honey until their bellies are full and their eyes go wild. "Leopard," says Nyomo, "give yourself a name. What name do you want to call yourself?"

"Strongman," says Leopard. "And you?"

"I'm Ironman," says Nyomo. "And Ironman is a better name than Strongman."

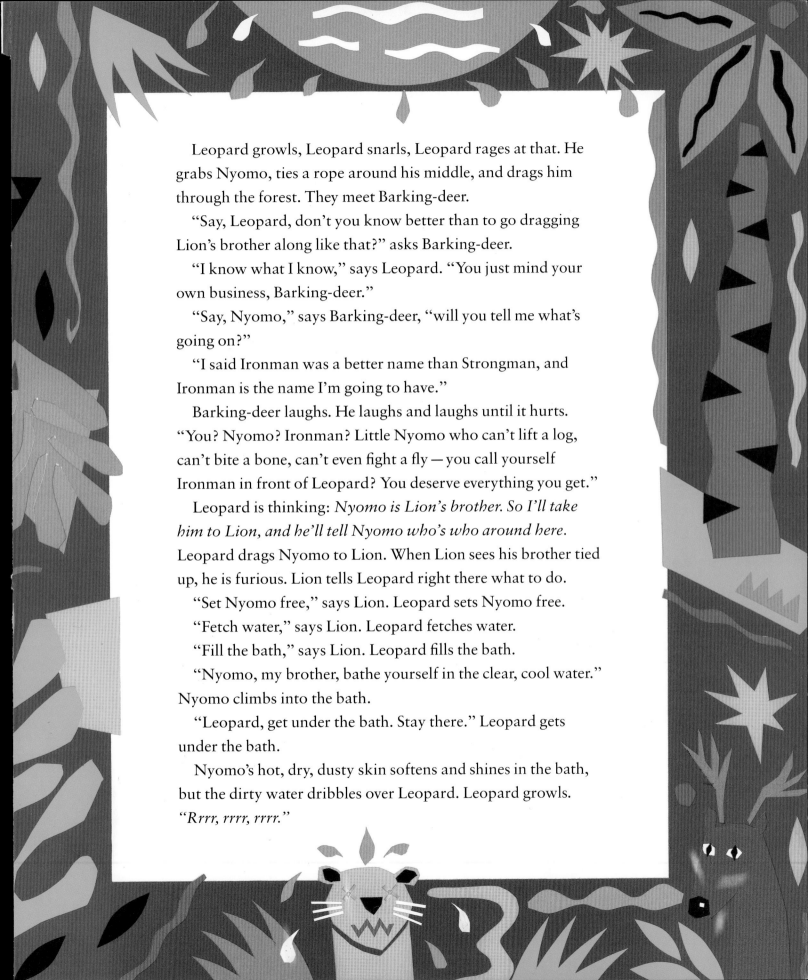

Leopard growls, Leopard snarls, Leopard rages at that. He grabs Nyomo, ties a rope around his middle, and drags him through the forest. They meet Barking-deer.

"Say, Leopard, don't you know better than to go dragging Lion's brother along like that?" asks Barking-deer.

"I know what I know," says Leopard. "You just mind your own business, Barking-deer."

"Say, Nyomo," says Barking-deer, "will you tell me what's going on?"

"I said Ironman was a better name than Strongman, and Ironman is the name I'm going to have."

Barking-deer laughs. He laughs and laughs until it hurts. "You? Nyomo? Ironman? Little Nyomo who can't lift a log, can't bite a bone, can't even fight a fly — you call yourself Ironman in front of Leopard? You deserve everything you get."

Leopard is thinking: *Nyomo is Lion's brother. So I'll take him to Lion, and he'll tell Nyomo who's who around here.* Leopard drags Nyomo to Lion. When Lion sees his brother tied up, he is furious. Lion tells Leopard right there what to do.

"Set Nyomo free," says Lion. Leopard sets Nyomo free.

"Fetch water," says Lion. Leopard fetches water.

"Fill the bath," says Lion. Leopard fills the bath.

"Nyomo, my brother, bathe yourself in the clear, cool water." Nyomo climbs into the bath.

"Leopard, get under the bath. Stay there." Leopard gets under the bath.

Nyomo's hot, dry, dusty skin softens and shines in the bath, but the dirty water dribbles over Leopard. Leopard growls. *"Rrrr, rrrr, rrrr."*

Now Nyomo rests. Lion and his wife bring food and sit and eat with Nyomo. They eat and eat and eat until all that's left is bits of bones, peels, and husks.

"Nyomo, dear brother," says Lion, pointing to the scraps. "Why not take these delicious little tidbits to Leopard?"

Nyomo takes the bits of bones, peels, and husks to Leopard. This drives Leopard into a roaring rage.

"Lion," roars Leopard, "I'll tear you into so many pieces, it'll take ten years to count the bits."

Lion doesn't move.

"Lion, I'll throw you so high, you won't come down until next year."

Lion doesn't move.

"Lion, I'll squash you so flat, you'll blow away on the wind like a leaf."

Lion moves. Lion rises. Lion pounces on Leopard; Leopard fights back. Biting, clawing, raging. Every piece Leopard bites out of Lion, he swallows. Every piece Lion bites out of Leopard he drops on the ground.

Then, see who's coming — Old Mother. She comes near. She sees Lion and Leopard locked together, fighting in the hot dust. She sees Lion tearing at Leopard. "Run Leopard!" she cries, "Run Leopard, before Lion kills you!"

So Leopard runs. He runs and runs until he finds a pool of cool mud. With his paws, he picks up clumps of mud, and, *fap, fap, fap*, he pats them into the holes Lion made. *Fap, fap, fap*, he closes them over until there are no holes left. Then Leopard lies down to get better.

Everything's fine for Leopard now, but his skin stays spotty forever.

PEACOCK

In the beginning, Peacock was just a dull, gray bird, and yet he went about boasting and bragging.

"I am the finest animal in India. In fact, I am the most magnificent creature on earth. You are all so fortunate to have the chance to cast your eyes upon me," he would say.

The other birds could not bear this talk, but they gathered around Peacock saying, "Peacock, you're fantastic. You're really beautiful, you know. So lovely to look at."

And Peacock would puff out his chest and strut about even more while the other birds flew off, fit to burst with laughter.

One day the birds made up a story.

"Peacock," they said, "out of all the birds in the jungle, we've chosen you to carry our best wishes to the lovely lady Ka Sngi who lives up, up, up in the Blue Kingdom of the Sky."

Peacock was delighted. "And what a good choice I am. Yes, it is I, Peacock, who has been selected to pay respects to Ka Sngi, she who pours out her bright light on us here on earth. I will win this great lady as my wife and live with her in the Blue Kingdom of the Sky."

The birds laughed among themselves. "Him! He's so fat he can hardly fly as high as a hedge!"

But Peacock said good-bye to them all and took off. Up, up, up he flew until he was out of sight. On he traveled until he landed at the dazzling palace of Ka Sngi, the lovely lady of the Blue Kingdom of the Sky.

Peacock bowed low. "I, Peacock, bring best wishes from all the birds on earth."

Happy Ka Sngi! All her life she had lived alone, and now, at long last, someone had come to see her.

"Oh come in, sir, you are more than welcome. Come live with me, and I will never be alone again."

She smiled, and her light shone out over all the world.

Peacock became her husband, but as every day passed, he became more selfish, more boastful, more demanding.

He spoke to Ka Sngi, saying, "Why should you, my wife, show so much care for the world, shining your light on those dull, ordinary creatures down there. You should shine all your light on me, Peacock."

Ka Sngi did what Peacock asked, and no light reached the earth. The whole world became dark and cold. The birds in the jungle stopped singing, and their feathers drooped.

Finally, they could stand it no longer and went to see a wise old woman.

She said to them, "All the people are in despair. Now that the earth is cold and dark, our crops won't grow. What little we have, you birds eat. All that I have left are a few mustard seeds. But listen! Promise me two things: stop eating my seeds and drive off the animals that eat my crops. If you do this, I will bring Peacock back to earth so we may all enjoy the light and warmth of Ka Sngi."

The birds agreed, and the wise old woman set to work. She planted her mustard seeds in the ground in the shape of a woman. The seeds sprouted, and when the flowers came out, it looked as if a beautiful golden lady lay on the ground.

Up in the Blue Kingdom of the Sky, Peacock looked down and saw the lovely golden lady.

He turned to Ka Sngi, saying, "Down on earth, I see there is a beautiful lady. I feel attracted to her, and I am sure if she were to see me, she would immediately fall madly in love with me. I can tarry here with you no longer."

Poor Ka Sngi! All her life she had lived alone, and now she was losing the only companion she had ever had.

"I beg you, stay! Stay!"

And as she pleaded with Peacock, she wept great tears. The drops fell on his dull, gray tail. The moment they touched his tail feathers, the tears became brilliantly colored spots.

Ka Sngi called after Peacock, saying, "These spots are a sign. Now you will never be able to forget me, Ka Sngi, the most beautiful and caring of women."

Peacock flew back to earth to meet the lovely golden lady on the ground.

"Ah, you birds, I am back. Would you be so kind as to convey me at great speed to see the golden beauty I observed from my palace on high?"

"Oh, yes, your majesty, we'd love to take you to see her," they said and took him to see the mustard flowers.

When Peacock saw that his lovely golden lady was nothing but a few flowers, he was struck dumb. He felt so foolish.

"Ah, but no matter," he said to himself, "there is always my beautiful Ka Sngi in the sky."

And so he started to flap his wings to fly back up to her. But Ka Sngi's tears weighed him down, and no matter how hard he tried and tried, he could fly no higher than a nearby tree.

And ever since that time, every morning, Peacock stretches his neck and flaps his wings to greet the coming of the light of Ka Sngi from her Blue Kingdom of the Sky. For the only happiness he can find here on earth is to spread his lovely feathers, marked with Ka Sngi's tears, so her light can shine on them.

CRANE

Princess Namirembe of Uganda sits in her father's great canoe.
Listen to the men who paddle:

> *"We are taking our Princess to the Island of Sese*
> *Where the sands are smooth and bright,*
> *The forests deep and dark,*
> *And the valleys cool and green.*
>
> *"See our paddles dive into the water,*
> *See our paddles fly out of the water,*
> *See our paddles shoot through the air."*

Princess Namirembe of Uganda sits in her father's great canoe,
longing to travel farther than the Island of Sese. Listen to her
father, the King:

> *"Wait, my daughter.*
> *Wait, watch, and learn before you travel*
> *To places far and wide where the ways are strange."*

Princess Namirembe of Uganda picks fruit in her father's
garden. Listen to the crane:

> *"Oh, Princess, come,*
> *Come to Kavirondo,*
> *Far away over the great lake*
> *To the wild country where the ways are strange.*
>
> *"Come, sit on my back,*
> *Hold onto my feathers — my wings will steady you —*
> *And close your eyes; for if you fall into the great lake,*
> *You will drown."*

Now Princess Namirembe of Uganda sits on the crane's back.
Listen to the crane:

"We are high in the sky,
  Above islands so small no one lives there
  But for diver birds, making their nests among the rocks.
  Nothing else but sky, water, and sun."

Princess Namirembe of Uganda waits in Kavirondo while the
crane flies off to visit his brother. Listen to the Princess:

"I see great dark hills
  And a plain stretching farther than my eye can see.
  Here I see warriors with helmets of cowrie shells,
  Ostrich feathers, and beads painted white, yellow, and red.
  White, yellow, and red beads on the women
  From a village that hides behind a fence of high, hard wood.

"Here there are no green hills
  As there are in my Uganda.
  Here there are no green banana gardens,
  No fruit trees, no grass, as there are in my Uganda."

Princess Namirembe of Uganda travels back to Uganda with the crane. Listen to the Princess:

"Oh, Father, I am back in beautiful Uganda with its lovely islands
And ripe crops glowing pink in the setting sun.
Let me tell you, oh, Father,
Where the crane took me. The ways were strange,
And the land was flat and dry,
Not like here in Uganda.
Uganda, I will never leave again."

Princess Namirembe of Uganda sits with her father and the crane. Listen to her father:

"You, oh, crane, I must thank
For showing my daughter other places
That make her happy to be here.
I have a gift for you,
A golden crest, dark at its root.
Take it and wear it wherever you go."

Listen to the storyteller tell you:

"Look now at the crane and see his golden crest, dark at the root.
Look now at the crane and see his golden crest, dark at the root."

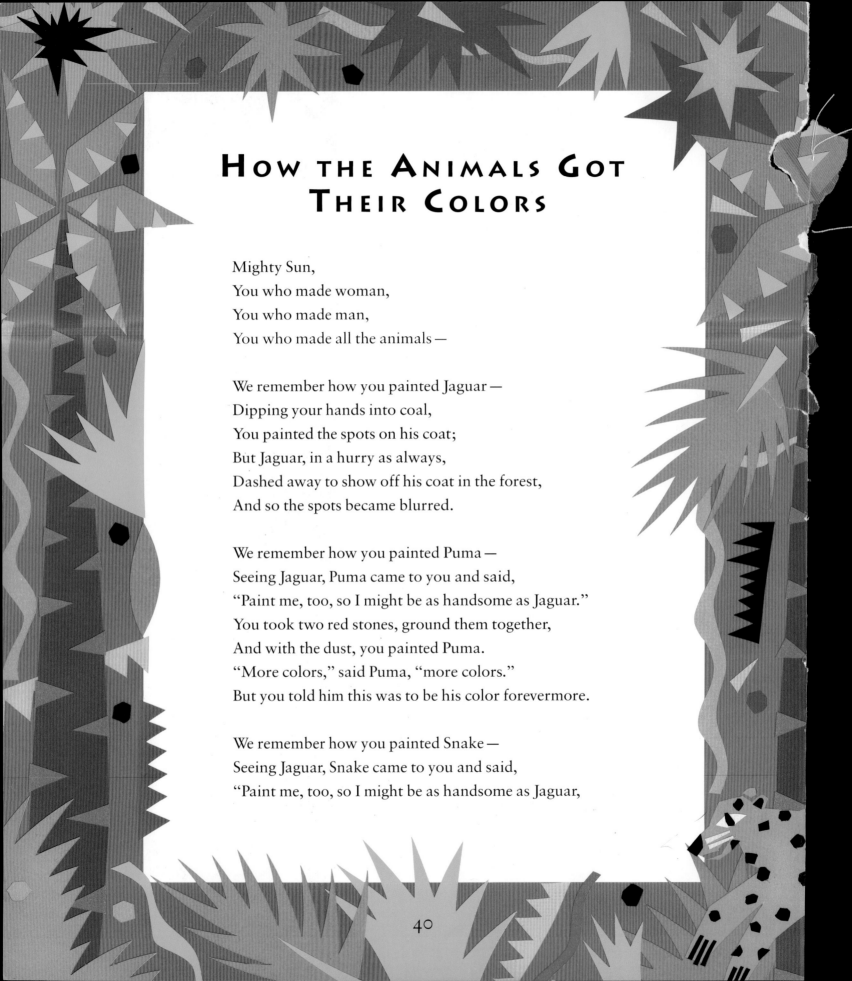

How the Animals Got Their Colors

Mighty Sun,
You who made woman,
You who made man,
You who made all the animals —

We remember how you painted Jaguar —
Dipping your hands into coal,
You painted the spots on his coat;
But Jaguar, in a hurry as always,
Dashed away to show off his coat in the forest,
And so the spots became blurred.

We remember how you painted Puma —
Seeing Jaguar, Puma came to you and said,
"Paint me, too, so I might be as handsome as Jaguar."
You took two red stones, ground them together,
And with the dust, you painted Puma.
"More colors," said Puma, "more colors."
But you told him this was to be his color forevermore.

We remember how you painted Snake —
Seeing Jaguar, Snake came to you and said,
"Paint me, too, so I might be as handsome as Jaguar,

But paint me brighter, paint me bolder."
You took a yellow stone, ground it to powder,
And with the powder, you rubbed Snake's skin.
Snake stretched herself, admiring her shining coils.

We remember how you painted Rat Snake—
Seeing Jaguar, Rat Snake came to you and said,
"Paint me, too, so I might be as handsome as Jaguar."
But you saw that you had no colors left,
And so you dipped your hands into the coal
And painted Rat Snake black all over.
Rat Snake smiled at the sight of her dark skin.

Mighty Sun,
You who made woman,
You who made man,
You who made all the animals—
This is how you painted the animals.

About These Stories

COYOTE

Coyote stories are told by various Native American tribes throughout the Southwestern United States. This particular coyote story is told by the Zuni. Many humorous tales are told about the coyote to help explain natural events and occurrences, social customs, and tribal ethics. Sometimes he plays tricks, and sometimes he is tricked. Stories about the coyote vary greatly, with some showing him as a buffoon, and some showing him as a god. These stories are most often told to children during the long winter.

The coyote lives on the western plains of North America. It can be four and a half to five feet long and feeds on rodents, insects, and fruit.

FLYING FISH

This story is told on the northeast coast of Papua, a province on the Pacific island of New Guinea. The folktales of this island are called *Vivarantua*. They are traditionally told to children by old women, and young married couples tell them to each other. A magic verse is recited before the telling of the story, and each story has a tune of its own. Many stories of the flying fish are told on this island.

Flying fish are found all over the warm waters of the world. They are about eight inches long and eat smaller fish.

FROG

This ancient Greek story was retold by the Roman poet Ovid in his book *Metamorphoses*. Latona (Leto in Greek) was a daughter of the Titans. She was loved by the Greek god Zeus and was forced to flee by his jealous wife, Hera. Afraid of Hera's anger, no one would help Latona, and she was left to wander forever. She gave birth to twins — the sun god Apollo and the moon goddess Artemis. The Greeks and Romans recited myths by heart at great public occasions. The tales were told in beautiful art and writing as well.

Frogs live on every continent except Antarctica. They range from one to twelve inches long and live in moist areas near water. They eat a variety of things, including insects, worms, and minnows.

TIGER

The Chu'an Miao who tell this tale live in the far north mountain region of China. They are a very old people, mentioned in the writings of the ancient Greeks. They love singing and storytelling at marriages, funerals, and at the eating of new grain. The tiger is found in many Asian myths. He is usually cunning and greedy. The dragon is spoken of in myths all around the world. In China, the dragon is said to hoard water and cause drought, especially in stories where she seeks refuge in the clouds.

The tiger lives in Asia in rain forests and mountains. It can be ten feet long and eats all kinds of meat, including buffalo and monkey.

BROLGA

The Brolga myth is told by the aborigines of Northern Australia. Aborigine tribal elders tell stories and make colorful paintings on rocks. These stories and paintings tell of the creation of the mountains, rocks, hills, fish, birds, and animals. They teach care and respect for nature. A harm done to the Brolga bird will offend her ancestor, who still dances on the plains.

The Brolga bird lives on the farmlands and wetlands of Northern Australia. It can grow to four and a half feet tall, and it eats fish and insects.

LEOPARD

Leopard's story is from the Loma tribe of the central mountains of Liberia, and it demonstrates tribal law and customs. Nyomo must be treated with respect, as he is the brother and honored guest of Lion, the most powerful animal of all. Liberia has three habitats — the seashore, the grasslands, and the mountains, and the tribes from each habitat tell very different stories.

The leopard lives in rain forests, grasslands, deserts, and mountains of Africa and Asia. It can grow to nine feet long and feeds on deer, baboons, monkeys, and other animals.

PEACOCK

The Khasi people, who tell this myth, live in the East
Khasi Hills of India. Many of their gods are female,
and they worship Ka Sngi, the sun goddess. The
Blue Kingdom of the Sky is a fabulous palace, home
of Mother Nature and her children — Ka Sngi (sun),
Ka Ding (fire), U Bnai (moon), and Ka Um (water).
The peacock is shown as pompous and fond of luxury in
many Indian myths. Each Khasi village has a very wise mem-
ber, such as the old woman in this story.

The Indian peacock lives in the rain forests of Ceylon and
India. It has a body length of about thirty inches and a tail
that spans five feet when spread. It eats seeds and green shoots.

CRANE

This myth comes from Uganda, in the Lake Region of East Africa.
Until the 1960s Uganda was part of a kingdom called Buganda.
Kings of Buganda were thought to have superhuman abilities,
such as the power to give the crane a crest. Myths were told
in dance and song by the elders as the tribe gathered around
a fire. A listener could journey far from everyday life into another
world (as the princess does in this story) and return refreshed and
happy. On Lake Victoria's southwestern coast there is a town called
Nyamirembe, and on the lake's western side are the Sese Islands.

The crowned crane is found in much of Africa on marshes,
plains, lakes, and seashores. About three feet tall, it eats small
animals, fruit, and roots.

HOW THE ANIMALS GOT THEIR COLORS

This is a myth of the Ayoreo Indians, who came from central South America in what is now Bolivia and Paraguay. This story is part of their creation myth, a myth that tells of the beginning of the world. The Ayoreo believe that heaven and earth were created by the sun god, who changed humans into animals and then gave the animals their colors.

The jaguar lives in South America, while the puma is found in North and South America. The jaguar can grow to eight feet long, and the puma ten feet long. They eat a variety of things, including deer and wild pig. The snake and the rat snake live in woodlands and farm buildings in North and South America, Europe, and Asia. They can grow to be four feet long and eat rats and mice.